The
RICKETT
HALL

Best wishes

Penny

Dora.

Other titles by Penny Dolan:

The Tale of

RICKETY HALL

Penny Dolan
Illustrated by Wilbert van der Steen

To my best brother Colin,
with much love and many memories.

Scholastic Children's Books,
Commonwealth House, 1-19 New Oxford Street,
London WC1A 1NU, UK
a division of Scholastic Ltd
London ~ New York ~ Toronto ~ Sydney ~ Auckland
Mexico City ~ New Delhi ~ Hong Kong

First published in the UK by Scholastic Ltd, 2000
This edition published by Scholastic Ltd, 2002

Text copyright © Penny Dolan, 2000
Cover illustration copyright © Klaas Verplancke, 2000
Illustrations copyright © Wilbert van der Steen, 2000

ISBN 0 439 98259 6

Printed and bound in Great Britain
by Cox & Wyman Ltd, Reading, Berkshire
Typeset in Horley Old Style

1 2 3 4 5 6 7 8 9 10

chapter 1

Once upon a winter night, snow began to fall. It drifted across the empty fields. It danced against the windows of the large lonely house high on the hill. Down swirled the snow around the streets of the town.

The soft flakes whirled in the wind, falling on everything – even on the two cloaked figures waiting in the shadows by the Market Square. Mr Megrim and his servant Filch, set on some wretched business.

Megrim's eyes burned above his upturned collar. His face twisted into a silent smile.

"Look!" he hissed.

There, over by the Market Steps, stood a thin boy without any coat and a small dog without any collar.

"I hates boys and I hates dogs," Megrim breathed, "and that pair will know it soon enough." His gloved hand closed around a leather lead. Filch raised a short thick stick and checked the sack hanging by his belt. Stealthily, Dog-Catcher Megrim and his man moved towards the boy and his dog.

The boy was Jonas Jones, and he was hardly more than skin and bones. Jonas had no family to care for him. He lived as best he could. Each night he sheltered where shelter was, and each day found him somewhere on the streets. His only friend was the small stubby-tailed mongrel called Scraps.

Sometimes Jonas found food for Scraps, and sometimes Scraps found food for Jonas. Often they had to beg by the Market Steps or starve. Nobody wanted them – nobody except Dog-Catcher Megrim, of course.

Megrim and Filch crept closer, under cover of the whistling wind. Suddenly Scraps's ears stood up, and his nose caught Megrim's strange smell. Scraps yelped a frantic warning.

There was a tangle of sacks and straps and sticks and shouts. Megrim grabbed and Filch snatched. Jonas wriggled and writhed and fought, and Scraps turned and twisted and growled. At last they slipped from Megrim's clutches and bolted into the safer darkness of the alleys.

"I hates boys and I hates dogs," Megrim bellowed after them, shaking his fist in rage. "I spy with my beady eye that doggie has no collar, laddie. He's nothing but a stray, and you're nothing but a vagrant – and I'll turn the key on you, so I will!" Megrim stamped off, with Filch following behind his master like an ill-formed shadow.

When all was quiet, Jonas and Scraps

crept out from under a stack of timber. By now the evening was even colder. The sleet stung them. The ice bruised them. Boy and dog were shivering fit to bust as they crossed the Market Square.

Jonas began to slide on the flagstones to warm himself. His battered boots raised ridges of silvery frost. Then, out of the snow, up jumped a piece of the ice – it flew in a bright jingling arc across the square and landed in the flickering light of a street lamp.

"A silver sixpence!" Jonas picked up the coin. "Here's luck right under our feet, Scraps! Tomorrow I'll buy you a collar and then that Dog-Catcher Megrim won't bother us no more." He tossed the coin in the air. "Reckon there'll be enough for a corking good dinner for us too!"

"Woof!" Scraps's short tail wagged eagerly.

chapter 2

To pass away the hours, Jonas and Scraps went up the High Street and down the Low Street. They peered in shop windows, searching for a collar to buy as soon as morning came.

The shops seemed the same – at first. They saw piles of buckets, pots and pails. They saw coils of rope and sacks of goods. They looked at rough aprons and thick gloves. They saw barrels and baskets, hutches and hen coops, blankets and boots. But not one shop had a collar or lead for sale.

"Most odd," said Jonas, his nose rubbed

raw by the freezing glass of the windows. "I wonder why. What do you think, Scraps?"

Then they turned a corner, and Jonas saw a new shop. It could not have been there long. The shop was full of things for dogs – but not good things. No bones or biscuits or bed-baskets, but strong collars and heavy leads and muzzles. Some had spikes and all had locks. Jonas peered at the prices.

He didn't know much about money, but every collar in that window was very, very expensive. They cost more than any ordinary person could pay. It was as if the shopkeeper did not want anyone to be able to afford a dog – not as a friend and pet, for sure.

Jonas shivered, but not with cold. He had a very bad feeling. There were things in that shop too nasty to think about. Jonas looked up. Across the top of the shop was a name, painted in twisted gold letters.

> MORTIASS MEGRIM Esquire,
> Dog-Catcher Extraordinary.
> Dog-Training A Speciality.
> Every Canine Question Solved.

Jonas stepped back in shock.

Then he heard a pitiful bark, then another, and another. The noises came from deep inside the shop. Scraps heard them too and whimpered. Jonas patted him comfortingly. It was a most unhappy sound.

Then, almost out of sight, in the corner of the shop window, Jonas spotted a small red collar. It would just fit Scraps, and it was the cheapest of all – one whole shilling!

"That's twelve-pennyworth," Jonas reckoned, sighing. "Six pence more." But he was determined to get that collar somehow. "I know what we'll do. We'll go singing round the houses. If folk fling us a few farthings, we'll have money for the collar in no time at all." Jonas wasn't sure about his idea, but he was going to try.

Together they went up the grand streets, around the middling streets and along the narrow streets. Jonas knocked at each door. He sang well enough, but folk rarely opened their doors to boys such as Jonas – especially on a freezing winter night.

"Stop that row!" people shouted. "Clear out! Go away!"

The doors stayed shut fast, keeping the warmth and the money inside.

Around and around Jonas and his dog wandered, and every moment they watched in case Megrim crept up on them. Soon there was not one single door they hadn't knocked on before. Jonas sat down wearily on the kerb, and stroked Scraps and patted his head. Jonas stared at the silvery stars in the dark sky, wishing something could be done.

He felt a sudden tingle run behind his ears, and an idea sing between them. "There's only one door we haven't knocked at, and that's the door of Rickety Hall," Jonas said. The words had come into his mind like magic.

For Rickety Hall was that old house high on the hill outside town. It was half hidden by trees. Nobody seemed to know who lived there, although sometimes lights glimmered through the dusty windows. No sound came from those silent stones – and certainly nobody ever went there. No one at all.

A hope and a boldness came into Jonas's

heart. "I don't care! I **will** go and knock at Rickety Hall tonight!" Jonas told Scraps fiercely. "They won't treat us worse than the folks down here."

"Woof!" agreed Scraps, as he scratched ice-drops from his ears. So, together, they set off through the snow, up the high hill.

chapter 3

Soon Jonas and Scraps stood at the entrance to Rickety Hall. Two iron gates creaked in the wind, and ivy clung to each gatepost. Scraps whimpered. His stubby tail drooped and his paws dragged. Jonas felt sorry for him.

"Stay here, behind this bush. You'll be quite safe," said Jonas, taking a length of old rope from his pocket. Quickly, he tied the little dog to a railing and walked away. "I'll be back soon, Scraps. Don't you worry." Jonas did not look back, even though he wanted to. He was rather scared himself.

All alone, Jonas walked up the long steep drive. Not one footprint had marked the deep snow ahead of him. Either side, the trees sang in the winter wind and owls hooted. Ahead stood the house, dark and mysterious, with one tall stone tower.

Jonas paused. He heard a rustling noise among the bushes, and then the padding of feet coming up behind him. He heard an urgent breathing.

Something's there! Jonas thought, and hurried on, trembling.

The sound grew closer, until it was right behind him. Jonas stepped out speedily, but his boot caught in a hole and he stumbled. In an instant something leapt on top of him.

"Aaah!" screeched Jonas. "It's the Demon of Doom!"

"Woof! Woof!" said Scraps, jumping around on Jonas and tangling him in a trailing rope. "Woof! Woof!"

Jonas cried with relief and joy. He ruffled Scraps's warm, rough fur and smiled to see that friendly stubby tail.

"You scared me out of my blooming wits!" Jonas told him. "Let's go on together."

They walked up the wide drive and past several strange-shaped bushes. Then, before them, stood Rickety Hall itself, silent as ever. A faint light was flickering somewhere behind the dusty windows, and a curl of smoke rose from each of the tall chimneys.

"I wonder who does live here," muttered Jonas, as Scraps moved ever closer to his side. "Still, they can't be worse than old meany Megrim, can they? If there's trouble, we run. Fast! All right?"

Jonas went up the stone steps of the great porch, took a breath and began his song. He lifted the heavy iron knocker and slammed it twice, hard, against the door. They heard the knock echo through the whole house. The little song seemed to hang in the air as Jonas and Scraps waited.

chapter 4

At last, soft footsteps came shuffling towards them. The great door creaked open. There stood an old man with bushy white hair and a thick white beard. His jacket was stained with inky patches.

"Aaaaah! By jings! It's a boy… a boy with a dog." The old man's voice creaked as if he had not spoken for years. He went quite wobbly with shock.

Quickly Jonas stepped forward, and helped the old man steady himself.

"No one has come to visit us for years and years," said the old man, shaking his head.

"There was that horrid big boy, years ago, who caused all the trouble…" he peered through his glasses at Jonas "…but you're not him. No, not at all. And such a nice little doggy! What a surprise! Come in."

Slowly the old man led them to a vast room, lit by flickering firelight. Jonas stared. There were books on shelves and tables, in heaps and stacks. Old certificates hung on the walls. A huge desk stood in the middle, covered with papers and inkwells and pens.

At the desk was a sturdy chair with wide wooden arms. Jonas helped the old man over to his seat.

As they reached the desk, a small well-chewed ball rolled out from among all the papers, and fell to the floor. Scraps, with a quick bark of joy, ran after it. The beardy old man watched the dog for a moment, and then turned to Jonas.

"Now, what is it you want, boy?" he smiled. His face was kind.

Jonas felt awkward, but unless he asked, he knew he would never get that collar for Scraps. He held out his hand.

"Please, sir, can I have a sixpence?"

The beardy old man paused. He scratched his head as if he had not decided about anything for years. Jonas waited. Scraps snuffled around with the ball, and rolled it with his paw. He nosed it towards the beardy old man.

"Oh, rickety-rackety! I can't say," the beardy old man said at last. "Talk turns to tales, so I'll speak nowt about owt. You'll have to go and ask my father." He pointed to the end of the corridor.

"Then I will. Thank you," Jonas said simply, setting off with Scraps pattering beside him.

* * *

So they did not see the beardy old man pick up the ancient leathery ball in his hand

and look at the teeth marks upon it, old and new. He sighed, as if he was remembering something lost long ago. He threw the ball up once and caught it. Then he rolled the ball gently across the floor, so that it skidded between the piles of books.

"Catch!" the old man whispered wistfully to the empty air.

chapter 5

Jonas and Scraps walked down a very long corridor. The carpet was worn and faded. Dusty patches showed that the walls had once been lined with paintings and cups. At the end was a carved door.

The next room was even larger than the first. It was full of paintings and statues, some half-finished. Clusters of candles flickered in the cold gusty air.

There, almost as if he was one of the statues himself, sat a very old man, half-dreaming. His hair and whiskers were as white as frost.

Around him lay sketches and drawings, curled with age, and pencils grey with dust. Nearby stood an easel and paints, but Jonas saw that the paintbrushes were stuck fast in dried jars.

"It's a bit brisk tonight," Jonas remarked. "You must be frozen, sir."

The fire in the hearth was dying away, so Jonas put a shovelful of coals in the grate. Scraps puffed and blew to make the cinders glow again. Jonas poked at the coals until the fire blazed out.

The very old man seemed to wake up when he heard the crackling of the flames. He turned to the fireplace and held his thin hands towards the leaping flames.

"That's better, isn't it?" Jonas said brightly.

Scraps was rolling around on the hearth-rug, giving short, gruff barks to show he was enjoying the warmth too. The very old man peered at Scraps, as if he was remembering something, or someone.

Then Jonas went to a large jug that stood by the window. He poured some water into each dry paint jar, whistling as he did so. Slowly, slowly, Jonas eased the paintbrushes free.

The very old man stared at Jonas with his two peery eyes. Then he stared at Scraps again. Then he smiled a long sweet smile and tottered over to the easel.

"Aha!" he said, and stretched his arms. He lifted one of the wet brushes, and put it to the paint.

"So, what do you want, boy?" His voice was soft, but kindly.

Jonas gulped and held out his hand. "Please, sir, can you give me a sixpence?"

The very old man's face clouded, and he sucked at the wooden end of the brush. "Oh, rickety-rackety! I can't say." He rubbed his chin. "Talk turns to trouble, so I'll speak nowt about owt. You'll have to go and ask my father." He pointed to a door. "Through there."

Another old man? "Ask your father?" Jonas gasped softly. "Well then, thank you, I will," he said, and set off again with Scraps.

* * *

So they did not see the very old man lower his easel and start to paint. Two furry ears and a furry nose... and two brown eyes...

a stubby tail… Rather like Scraps, but not exactly like him.

"Ah!" smiled the very old man rather sadly. "Such a silly old sausage, I remember…"

chapter 6

Ahead was a vast stone staircase. Silence seemed to gather around that stairwell. A chandelier, covered in cobwebs, hung from the far-off ceiling. Up they went, the boy and the small dog.

Soon they came to another door, half open, and through it they went. They were in a room full of the most curious things.

Weird wooden carvings were piled high in the corners. Strange weapons were fastened to the walls. There were objects from far-off lands and far-off times. Stuffed animals and birds gazed silently from glass cases. An enormous wooden canoe, full of odd-shaped bundles, lay on the floor.

By the canoe sat a very, very old man, even older than the one before, and his hair was as white as snow. This extremely old man had a patterned blanket around his shoulders. He sat as silently as any of the mysterious animals. His thin finger pointed to the maps spread across his lap, as if he was trying to trace distant journeys, but had lost his way. The extremely old man gave a very soft sigh.

"Excuse me. I think I can help you, sir," said Jonas. He had spotted a magnifying glass, tucked beneath the extremely old man's chair.

Jonas knelt down and pulled the glass free. He found a cloth and cleaned the round lens, and then he put it in the outstretched hand. The extremely old man smiled. Slowly he lowered the magnifying glass and held it a little above the map. He made a small satisfied noise and nodded his head. "Just as I thought!" he said. "Most interesting."

Then he lifted the glass and gazed through it at Jonas, up and down. "Aha! I spy a real boy – and a nice boy at that," he said. "Not like that sneaky what's-his-name." Then he spotted Scraps, pattering among the fearsome animals, growling and barking up at them as if they were real.

"And a dog – a real live dog again. At last! So what do you want, boy?" The extremely old man's voice was faint but kindly.

Jonas gulped and held out his hand. "Please, sir, can you give me a sixpence?"

The extremely old man said nothing for a while. Then he tutted. "Oh, rickety-rackety! I can't say. Talk turns to tittle-tattle so I'll speak nowt about owt. You'll have to ask my father." He pointed to the foot of a wooden staircase. "He's up there."

"Then I will," Jonas smiled, and somehow this time he was not so astonished. He thanked the extremely old man, and set off with Scraps to clamber up the steep stairs.

So they did not see the extremely old man look at the great grizzly bear. It was the one that little Scraps had growled at. They did not see him chuckle to himself, and turn to an old photograph on the wall, a photo from long ago.

"Ah! What a brave doggy you were!" he mumbled to the faded image. "How I wish..." he began, but his voice trembled away to nothing.

chapter 7

Up went Jonas and Scraps. The wooden staircase leant this way and that. It twisted higher and higher inside Rickety Hall, and all the time the air seemed to grow as quiet as quiet. At last they reached a thin elegant door.

Jonas and Scraps stepped through into a forest of musical instruments – tall harps, fat cellos, silvery flutes, round drums, delicate violins and tottering stacks of music.

In the midst of all this sat an exceedingly old man in an ornate armchair. His hair hung in thin strands on the shoulders of his old-fashioned coat. He held a thin baton between his bony fingers.

Beside him was an ancient gramophone with a wind-up handle, and a big brass trumpet for a speaker. A black record was going round and round, but not one sound came out. The exceedingly old man had his eyes closed, and he was frowning crossly.

Jonas went over and coughed loudly. The exceedingly old man looked quite fearful to see a boy and a dog beside him.

Jonas gave his most friendly smile. "Excuse me, sir, but I might be able to help you. Don't worry."

Jonas reached inside the hollow speaker trumpet and pulled. Out came a pair of old socks, a squashed tea cosy, two stale buns, the head of a feather duster, several crumpled manuscripts and a very deaf mouse. Loud music filled the room, washing into every corner, and happy voices carolled out hallelujahs as joyfully as could be.

The exceedingly old man gave a blissful smile. "Oh! Oh!" he said, and his eyes filled with tears.

Scraps padded over and sat listening attentively to the gramophone's wonderful sound. His stubby tail beat time until the music stopped.

"So, now you have helped me, how can I help you? What do you want, boy?" asked the exceedingly old man.

"Please, sir," said Jonas, "can I have a sixpence?"

"Oh dear!" the exceedingly old man said, shaking his head. "Rickety-rackety, I don't know. Talk turns to teasing so I'll speak nowt about owt." He pointed to a narrow door. "You'll just have to go and ask my father."

"Then," sighed Jonas, "I will. Thank you." He and Scraps went on.

* * *

So they did not see the exceedingly old man pick up an ancient record. On the faded paper cover was a picture of another dog, listening to a gramophone. Scraps had sat in just the same way, with his head on one side. The exceedingly old man smiled, and set the gramophone playing once more.

chapter 8

Jonas and Scraps clambered up a narrow flight of wooden stairs. At last they came to a high-up room. In the room was a vast four-poster bed, hung with curtains. In the bed lay an unbelievably old man, even older than the others.

His face was as wrinkled as a walnut, and a tuft of white hair sprouted from his head. His eyes were half-closed, as if he were dreaming.

Suddenly there was a gust of wind, and a window blew open. Wintry leaves fluttered in, scattering the foot of the bedspread.

Jonas went over and shut the window-latch. Then, carefully, he lifted the leaves off the bed. As Jonas did this, he sang a small comforting tune, so that the old man would not be alarmed. Scraps stood on his hind legs and put his paw on the bedspread.

The unbelievably old man stirred and began to hum too. He hummed along with Jonas. He opened his eyes and smiled up at them. Then he reached out a wrinkled hand and felt for Scraps's soft paw.

"Good Fido," he said in a voice no more than a whisper. "Good dog." Scraps licked the outstretched hand.

The unbelievably old man looked at Jonas in a dreamy sort of way. "A boy – and a dog with him. A kind boy, at long last. What do you want, boy?" he asked.

Jonas gulped, and held out his own hand. For a moment he did not like to ask, but really he had no choice. "Please, sir, can you give me a sixpence?"

The unbelievably old man lay silent. Jonas thought he had gone off to sleep, but then he gave a deep breath and spoke. "Oh, rickety-rackety! I can't say." Jonas leant closer to hear the whispered words. "I'll speak nowt about owt for it's safer that way." The old man fell silent.

Jonas felt his heart sink. So this was it? Had he been wasting his time? Then the old man wheezed and spoke once more.

"You'll just have to go and ask my father. He's..." he pointed a quivery finger to the foot of a small ladder that reached up through a hole in the floor. "...up there."

Jonas's mouth dropped open. He could not believe anyone older even existed. Then he spoke firmly. "I will. I must," he said. "Thank you. Come on, Scraps."

chapter 9

Jonas climbed up the rickety-rackety ladder, and Scraps scrabbled up the rungs behind him. At last they stood in a high white room at the very top of Rickety Hall.

The floor was totally bare. There was no chair, or table or bed. Windows were set on all sides, and through them, Jonas saw the bright stars shining in the night sky. His heart sank.

Then he noticed that a high shelf ran all around the room. On that shelf stood an ancient, upturned hat. Jonas stood on tiptoe, and carefully lifted it down.

Jonas peered down into the hat. He did not see a scarf, or a pair of gloves tucked inside. Instead, there, on a small cushion of soft wool, under a warm blanket, lay the oldest old man in the whole wide world. His eyes were tightly shut. He lay so still that Jonas did not want to wake him.

Jonas was just about to put the hat back when the oldest old man of all opened two bright eyes and looked straight at him.

"What do you want, Jonas Jones?" His voice was as clear as a bell.

At first, Jonas was so surprised he could not answer. At last he spoke. "Please, sir, can I have a sixpence? I need to buy a collar to keep my little dog safe," he explained shyly.

The oldest old man of all gave a tiny chuckle, and the hat shook slightly in Jonas's arms. Then he winked one bright eye at Jonas.

Slowly, from under the warm blanket, he stretched out a weeny wrinkled fist. Then his weeny wrinkled fingers opened one by one, and there in the oldest old man's palm lay a shining silver sixpence.

"YES, JONAS JONES!" said the oldest old man of all. "Take your sixpence at last, and may you and your dog have all the luck you need!"

Jonas took the coin. "Thank you very much, sir," he said. "I hope we will."

"Now lift me back again, Jonas!" ordered the oldest old man of all. Carefully Jonas put the hat back on to the shelf, and tiptoed out of the room.

Jonas and Scraps clambered down the ladder. Then they ran through every room, one after another, calling and barking happily.

"Thank you all. Look after each other, won't you?" Each old man watched Jonas and Scraps pass by. For a moment all was quiet. It seemed as if the silence was enfolding the house in its depths again.

Then the old men called out, all together. "Yes, we will," they said. "And you look after yourself, Jonas Jones."

Somewhere, an ancient clock stirred, and whirred a little. Then it started to tick – a little faintly at first – and then to strike. The cheerful chime of that clock rang strong and sweetly through every corner of every room in Rickety Hall.

* * *

So now Jonas, with his two sixpences tucked tightly in his pocket, stood under the carved porch once more.

He shook the hand of the beardy old gentleman who had first opened the door, and thanked him once more.

"Wait!" The beardy old man reached into his pocket for the ball that Scraps had found earlier. He gave it to the little dog. Scraps took the ball in his mouth and wagged his tail. The beardy old man stroked behind the little dog's soft ear.

"I knew a little dog just like you once upon a time," he said. "Once. Goodbye, Scraps. Goodbye, Jonas."

Then, blinking his eyes, he shut the huge door, and they heard his feet shuffling away down the corridor.

chapter 10

Jonas and Scraps were all alone once more. It was still chilly, even though the night had turned towards morning. They trod slowly across the snow-covered ground, towards the strangely shaped hedges. They were thinking about the strange family of old men left behind inside Rickety Hall.

Then it seemed to Jonas that one of the shadowy bushes moved. And then another. Suddenly, out of the night sprang Megrim and Filch with a large net.

"Got you!" gloated Megrim.

"Got you!" echoed Filch.

"Help!" yelled Jonas. "Help! Help!"

"Arf! Arf!" barked Scraps. "Arf!"

Megrim and Filch wound them tightly into the ropes of the net. Jonas knew that there was no escape.

Megrim sneered down. "I'll find the worst workhouse in the world for you, laddie, and even worse than that for your little doggie," he scoffed. "I said I'd catch you in the end!"

Jonas fumbled around and thrust the two sixpences through the net. "Please, Mr Megrim," he begged. "Here's a shilling for the red collar in your shop window. Please let Scraps go. Please."

Megrim took the two coins, and tucked them away tightly inside his own coat.

"You stupid boy! Now I've two silver coins and you've got none. Your nasty little dog is done for," Megrim chuckled horridly. "And so are you."

"Help!" called Jonas, from under the net.

"Arf! Arf! Arf!" cried Scraps from under Jonas.

"It's no good you wretches calling out!" Megrim leered. "No one will help you here. Let's go."

Megrim and Filch began to drag the bundle along the snowy ground.

"Oh, we hates boys and we hates dogs. Oooooh – how we hates 'em!" guffawed the two villains, tugging at their helpless bundle.

Suddenly, the huge door of Rickety Hall opened. Out burst five old men, strong and sprightly with rage.

"We will!" they cried. "We'll help them!"

The old men were armed with the ancient bats and hockey sticks. They circled around Megrim and Filch waving their weapons threateningly.

"I know those beady eyes," cried the first old man, his beard bristling with fury. He pointed at Megrim's face. "And they're not to be trusted."

"I know that meany nose," said the very old man. "That pokes around in other people's business."

"And I know that horrid smile," called the extremely old man. "It's as full of fibs as it is of teeth."

"It's meany Morty Megrim!" they shouted. "Twice as big and ten times as nasty!"

Jonas and Scraps peered out from the folds of the net, trying to see what was going on.

"Morty's the boy we took into our house, and he paid us by scaring all our dogs away." The beardy old man's face was white with anger. "Morty's the boy who crept from room to room telling tales and tittle-tattling."

Megrim and Filch stared, bewildered, as the furious old men danced around.

"I remember," declared the extremely old man, stamping his foot, "how he twisted our words to make mischief and trouble between us."

"He set us against each other…" muttered the exceedingly old man, lashing about with his baton.

"…So we'd say nowt about owt, and not a word to each other," ended the unbelievably old man, his nightcap bobbing.

"But no more – no, nay, never, no more!" they cried. "No more of nowt. Now we'll speak out, and we'll shout all about – about you, Morty Megrim, that's who!"

The beardy old man pointed at Filch. "And you're nothing but a fool, copying this villain and his wicked ways. Have you no mind of your own?" Filch's mouth hung loose and his eyes grew puzzled.

"Haul, Filch!" ordered Megrim, moving into action. "Haul the net away." Filch hesitated, trembling.

"NO! NO! NO! He'll not have our boy, or our little dog! He'll not spoil things again!" the old men cried. "One for all and all for one – and that one's Jonas Jones," they yelled. "Tally ho! Down with the vile villains." Blows rained on Megrim and Filch. "Rogues and rapscallions – take that! Let go!" they yelled.

Megrim and Filch dropped the net, and flew down the drive. Quick as a fish, Jonas slithered out of the net, and Scraps wriggled out after him. They scrambled to their feet.

"Hooray!" cheered the old men, hugging and patting them to make sure they were safe and sound. Then they all turned after Megrim and Filch.

chapter 11

To their surprise, there were no fleeing figures on the steep and slippery drive. Instead, two shapes were tumbling downwards through the snow, growing larger and rounder with each turn.

Gradually, the shapes became two giant snowballs, rolling rapidly down the drive. Over and over they went, faster and faster, until with two tremendous thuds the snowballs crashed against the mighty gateposts of Rickety Hall.

"Ow!" yelled the largest heap. "Ow! Ow! And now I hates snowballs too."

The two villains crawled painfully out of their snowy mounds and sat rubbing their heads and knees.

"Megrim and Filch! Mark my words!" called the beardy old man. Now his voice was not soft and kindly. It echoed with anger across the frosty air. "You two are nothing but cruel, common thieves. If you don't leave this place..."

"And that shop..!" shouted Jonas.

"And this town..!" shouted the other old men, "...we will bring the law down on you!"

The roaring of the old men seemed to set the treetops a-quivering.

"Ha! There's nothing you can do to me," laughed Megrim, standing upright once more. "Not to me – the **Great Mortiass Megrim, Dog-Catcher Extraordinary!**" he yelled as loud as he could.

At the sound of Megrim's triumphant cry, there was a sharp cracking noise. Snow came from everywhere – falling from the branches, gathering from the bushes, tumbling from the tree-trunks, rumbling from the gulleys until it rushed down the hill like a fall of white water.

Megrim and Filch turned and fled, but the avalanche seemed to gather them into its icy grip. In a moment, it had crashed over the steep sides of Rickety Hill, down into the darkness.

Jonas looked at the little old men. They shook their heads, but their eyes were bright and they smiled with the joy of victory.

"Hooray," they cried. "The boy's safe and the little dog is safe!"

Scraps wagged his tail and danced and Jonas laughed aloud too, and the old men hugged him. He was just wishing that maybe the old men might say something more to him, something very important indeed. The old men paused, as if they were about to speak.

Then Jonas suddenly remembered the mournful howling and barking he had heard earlier that night. His face fell.

"But," Jonas asked, "what about all the other dogs?"

"What other dogs?" The old men glanced around, looking under the bushes and hedges.

"The dogs who are in the back of Megrim's shop," he explained. "What will happen to them now? Who is going to look after them?" Jonas worried. "I must go and find them," he said.

"Not by yourself!" the old men cried. "Wait a moment, Jonas Jones!"

chapter 12

A short while after, as the morning sun set the snow glistening, a sledge set off from Rickety Hall.

The sledge went scooting and shooting all the way down to the town. At the back sat Jonas and Scraps. At the front, wrapped in a great warm coat was the beardy old man. After a wiggle or two, he was steering the old sledge as if he did it daily.

Megrim's shop was silent and dark, but the door was not locked. Cruel muzzles and traps and chains lay scattered around. It was a horrid place. Scraps sniffed and whined.

"This way," Jonas called, and hurried through a curtained doorway.

At the back of the shop they found a yard. There, chained and filthy, were the dogs – those who could bark, and those who were silently waiting to die.

Empty crusted dishes lay here and there. One or two dogs were licking thirstily at the melting snow. They were covered in sores.

"Oh!" said the beardy old man, shaking his head. "Oh dearie me!"

"What can we do?" said Jonas.

The poor creatures seemed starved – almost skin and bones. Jonas knew how their hunger felt. He was in tears.

The beardy old man frowned for a while. "First," he said, "the dogs must be cared for." He took a small notepad out of a pocket, and began to scribble something down. "We'll need a horse and cart to carry the poorly dogs. We'll need medicines and ointments and plenty of food."

The beardy old man scratched his head. "I will need you to deliver these messages, Jonas. This horrid shop must be closed, and the poor dogs brought up to Rickety Hall as soon as possible."

Jonas looked at the dogs. There were large dogs and little dogs, and dogs in between – all different kinds and colours.

"You'll have all of them?"

"Yes! Unless any owners ask for them, of course. There'll be dogs everywhere – in the barn, in the garden, in the yard, in the house – just like the old days!" the old man cried. "Once we had lots of dogs at Rickety Hall." He stopped suddenly, and seemed very sad. "But maybe not…"

"Whatever's the matter?" cried Jonas.

"Maybe the dogs shouldn't come to us. Maybe we are all too old to give these dogs a home," the beardy old man mused. Then he winked. "Unless, Jonas, you'll come to Rickety Hall too and help us? We need a boy like you about the place."

"Woof? Woof?" Scraps gave a small sad bark.

"Of course, Scraps, you too!" the old man smiled through his beard."What do you say, Jonas Jones?"

Now Jonas Jones had no father to ask, and so he should have been able to answer for himself, and he could have answered for himself – but he didn't.

Because, before Jonas could open his mouth, Scraps jumped at the beardy old man, wagging his tail for all he was worth. "Woof! Woof! Woof!"

And that was answer enough.

chapter 13

So Jonas Jones stayed on at Rickety Hall with his new family. He was kept busy, looking after all the old men and all the dogs.

Jonas gave every dog good food: just a little at a time at first, until they were used to it. He found each one a comfy place to sleep. He looked after their bruises and sores until they were quite healed. He took the dogs for small walks, then for longer walks, and then out for runs until they were sleek and strong again.

As for the old men, they looked after Jonas too, so he also grew happy and healthy and strong. They had so many interesting stories to tell that Jonas grew up learning all sorts of amazing and wonderful things.

It was strange too, that, out of the many animals who came to the house on the hill, each old man found one dog to be his own special pet – or was it that each of those dogs had found one special old man? Jonas was never sure.

As for Rickety Hall, with the noise of the old men chattering, the dogs playing, and the many visitors gasping at the interesting rooms – well, it never seemed silent or sad again. Hour by hour and day by day, the ancient clock struck with a sweet, sure sound.

Nevertheless, sometimes Jonas and Scraps sneaked out and went for quiet walks by themselves, and remembered what they wanted to remember.

* * *

One midsummer day, when the grass swished softly against them as they walked, they came to the big stone gates at the foot of the hill.

"Woof!" Scraps sniffed, and began to dig urgently. Jonas looked to see what the little dog had discovered. In the ground lay two silver coins thrown from a passing pocket one snowy long-ago night.

"The silver sixpences!" cried Jonas, beaming. He stared thoughtfully at them. Then he pushed the earth and grass back into place over them. "We've luck enough at Rickety Hall, Scraps. We'll leave them for someone else to find."